THE LITTLE GIRL WHO WANTED TO BE BIG

To Alice,
for always inspiring me to think big.

Credits: Amber Dusick made the ceiling drawings; Maria Serfontein made the pajamas;
Alice's great grandmother, the late Betty Rose Faries, made the teddy bear.

Special thanks to Alice and Jen for their patience and professionalism, and to my mom, Peggy Engledow, for
her portrayal of "Grandma" on page 9.

All photography by Dave Engledow, except for the following:
Ama Dablam, pg 32, climbers, pg 32, whale, pg 33, used under license from Shutterstock.com; roller coaster,
pg 5, ocean surface, ocean bottom, cargo ship, pg 33, used under license from iStock.com; Jupiter, Mercury,
Venus, Mars, Earth, Moon, Milky Way, spiral galaxy, pp 34–40, courtesy NASA/JPL-Caltech.

ISBN: 978-0-06-242539-3

The artist used software to manipulate the composite photographs for this book.
Design by Chelsea C. Donaldson and Honee Jang
18 19 20 21 22   SCP   10 9 8 7 6 5 4 • ❖ • First Edition

THE LITTLE GIRL WHO WANTED TO BE BIG

DAVE ENGLEDOW

HARPER

An Imprint of HarperCollinsPublishers

There once was a little girl
who wanted to be big.

Everyone was always telling her she was too little to do the things she wanted to do—like cooking breakfast by herself . . .

. . . or helping Grandma with the yardwork.

"Hit the brakes, dear—you're going WAY too fast."

The little girl tried everything she could think of to get bigger.

She put on platform shoes.

She did strengthening and stretching exercises.

She ate *all* the broccoli at dinner.

But nothing worked.

"When will I be able to do big things?" she asked Dad.

"If you want to do big things, you have to think big," he replied.

"But how do I think big?"

she asked Mom.

"If you want to think big, you need to dream big," Mom said. "Stay focused, always keep your eye on the big picture, and big things are bound to happen."

That night, the little girl never once took her eye off the big picture.
She was certain big things were about to happen.

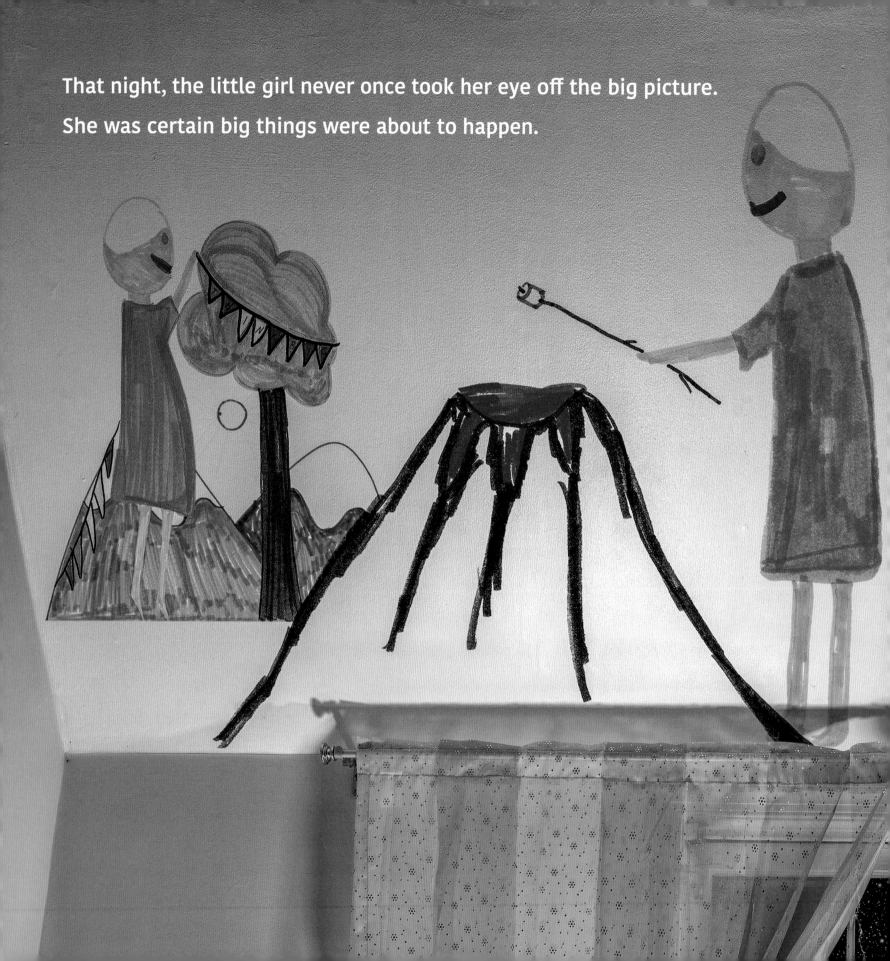

The early morning sun woke the little girl from her happy dreams. "I have a feeling today is going to be a *VERY BIG* day!"

"You are what you eat!" she said before diving into the biggest breakfast she'd ever had.

"That's it, Mom! Stay focused on the big picture."

"Good-bye, car seat! I'm a big kid now!"

But the little girl wasn't satisfied with just *being* big. She also wanted to *do* big things . . .

. . . like helping Mom and Dad around the house . . .

. . . lending a hand

in the community . . .

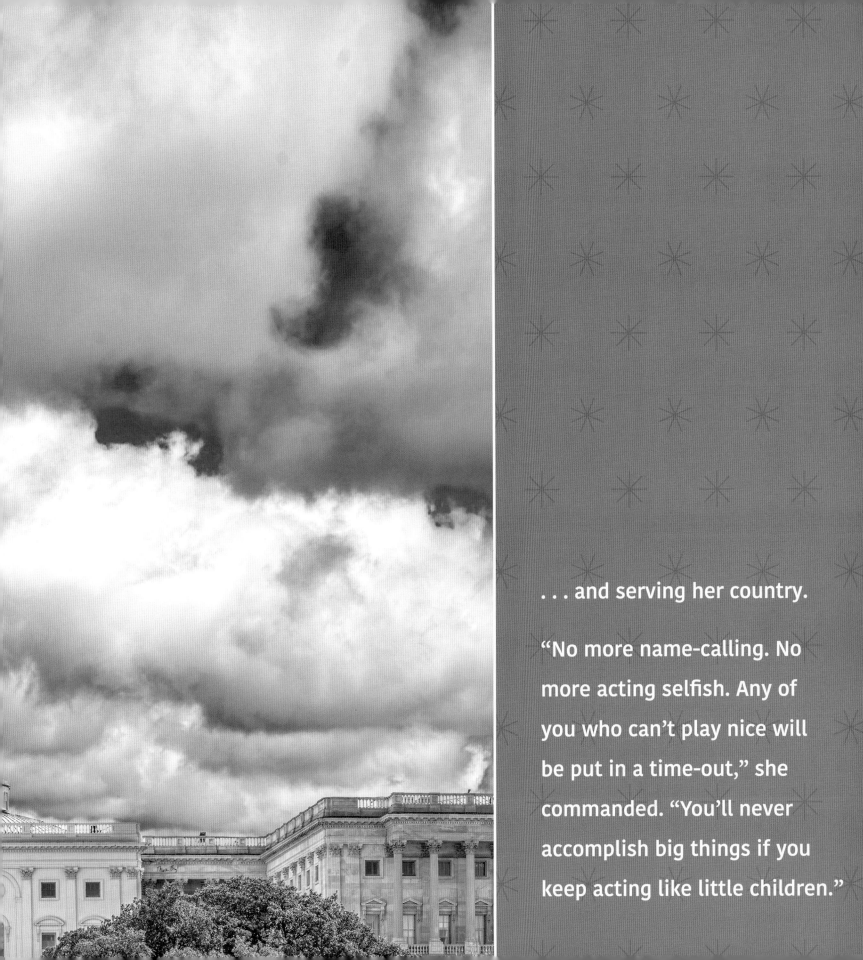

. . . and serving her country.

"No more name-calling. No more acting selfish. Any of you who can't play nice will be put in a time-out," she commanded. "You'll never accomplish big things if you keep acting like little children."

For the big little girl,

no mountain was too high . . .

. . . no ocean too deep . . .

. . . no planet too far.

And just like that, the little girl was the biggest person who had ever lived. But the bigger she became, the more she missed the little things . . .

. . . like story time on Mom's lap, riding up high on Dad's shoulders, and her comfy, cozy bed back home.

So she decided to do something about it.

"Think big," she reminded herself as she wished on every star in the galaxy.

"Welcome home," she said to Mom and Dad.

"Get some sleep, because tomorrow's going to be a *VERY BIG* day."